The Genie
of the
Bottle Bank

SEAN TAYLOR

Illustrated by Ella Okstad

ALFORD PRIMARY SCHOOL

CHAPTER 1
Pigsty

"Look at you two!" said Mum. "It's a lovely day and all you do is sit around watching television!"

Uh-oh, thought Arthur, glancing across at Dad, here we go.

It was the same every weekend. Mum and Dad always found some reason to start shouting at each other.

"Hang on, pet," said Dad, holding up a hand. "This is the most exciting part of the film."

"You've been saying 'Hang on, pet, this is the most exciting part of the film' all afternoon!" snapped Mum.

"But it is," said Dad, stretching out lazily.

"That man's about to make himself invisible …" said Arthur, pointing at the television.

"I don't care if he's about to pull a kangaroo out of his ear," said Mum. "I just wish you'd stop gawping at the television like two cows staring at a cabbage! It's a lovely, sunny day outside!"

"Then why don't you go outside?" suggested Dad.

"I've been outside all day," said Mum. "And so have all the other dads in the street. They've been mowing their lawns, cleaning their cars and building climbing-frames for their children …"

"Mum's right," said Arthur. "Last week, Warren's dad built a tree-house, with a door and windows that open and close."

"Well, Warren's dad is a builder," yawned Dad. "I don't know how to do that sort of thing."

"You don't even know how to change a light-bulb," said Arthur, with a little smile.

"I've changed more light-bulbs than you've had hot dinners," said Dad.

"Well, I asked you to change the one in my bedroom about three weeks ago, and you haven't done it yet," said Arthur.

"You know I'm scared of heights," sighed Dad.

"A light-bulb isn't high!" said Arthur.

"It is for me," said Dad. "And that stepladder we've got is wobbly. It's like trying to stand on top of a jellyfish."

"How on earth would you know what it's like up that ladder?" said Mum. "You haven't used it for about eight years! It's buried under all that junk in the garage."

"It's like a pigsty in there," said Mum. "I can't imagine what the neighbours must think. The least you could do is sort that lot out."

"All right, all right," said Dad, looking away from the television for the first time.

"Mmm," said Mum, narrowing her eyes. "Well, I'm going to pick up the new living-room curtains. Let's see what you manage to do by the time I get back. If it's more than make yourself a cheese sandwich, I'll be amazed."

"That's a good idea," said Dad with a little wink. "Do you fancy a cheese sandwich, Arthur?"

Arthur heard Mum drive off. Then he went into the kitchen and found Dad carefully making two cheese sandwiches.

"Are you going to tidy up the garage for Mum?" he asked.

"Will you give me a hand?" replied Dad. "We can get that garage looking spick and span in no time."

Arthur nodded and bit into his sandwich. A little while later, they were pulling open the stiff door into the garage. Inside it smelt of old string and flowerpots.

"It *is* like a pigsty," said Arthur, squeezing past a pile of old paint-pots.

Dad shrugged and peered into a box containing one roller-skate, half a guitar and a bird's nest.

"I don't think many pigs would want to live in a place like this," he sighed.

"What are we going to do with it all?" asked Arthur.

"Chuck it out," said Dad. "These paint brushes are no good any more, and these wellies look as though a donkey's been

trying to eat them."

Dad started handing old planks, broken tiles and other things to Arthur, who made a pile of rubbish in the garden.

"We'll take it all down to the tip later," yawned Dad, reaching into a wooden box and pulling out three old bottles.

"These were your grandad's," he said, holding them up to the light. "But there's no point in keeping them now."

"I could take them to the bottle bank on the corner," said Arthur.

"Good idea," said Dad, handing him the bottles. "That'll save a few trees."

Arthur gave him a funny look.

"You're mad!" he said.

"Why's that?" asked Dad, sitting down on an upturned box in the doorway.

"Bottles aren't made from trees!" said Arthur, setting off out into the street.

"No?" shrugged Dad. "Well, recycling them must be saving something. Perhaps it's whales."

Arthur walked away, shaking his head.

"Come straight back," called Dad.

"I will," said Arthur.

"And when you drop the bottles in, make sure you don't fall in after them!"

Arthur looked at the bottles as he carried on down the pavement. Two of them were an ordinary shape, but the third was wide and round. It had funny little handles

coming out of its sides, and a cork in the
top that was so old it had gone black.
Arthur decided that was the one that was
going to make the biggest smash.

He got to the bottle bank and pushed the
first bottle through the hole.

Down it fell. CRASH!

Down fell the second. SMASH!

Arthur smiled at the funny bottle. It only just fitted through the hole. And when it dropped inside …

KAAAAAARACK-BOOM!!!

It was like a bomb going off. The ground seemed to tremble.

Arthur put his hands over his head, and his nose filled with a smell of cheesy socks. When he opened his eyes, he saw green smoke billowing out of the bottle bank.

Arthur wanted to turn round and run, but before he could, the strangest thing happened. The green cloud started growing darker and gathering together.

Arthur was frozen to the spot, and watched in amazement as the smoke began to form a shape.

At first it seemed to be turning into an enormous green rugby ball.

Then it began to look like a huge green seal. And finally, it became … a large, smiling genie.

CHAPTER 2
Your Wish is My Command

"Woooh!" yawned the genie, giving a huge stretch. "Ooooh! Thank goodness for that. My friend, you've no idea the pins and needles you get when you're stuck inside a little bottle."

Arthur stared up at the genie, not really knowing what to say, so he asked, "What's that smell?"

The genie looked down at his feet. "Well, your socks would smell cheesy if you hadn't changed them for nine thousand years!"

"Nine thousand years?"

"That's how long I was stuck inside that little bottle."

"What did you do for nine thousand years?" asked Arthur.

"Well," said the genie. "I spent quite a lot
of it thinking about what I was going to
have to eat when I got out."

"And what's that?"

"One of my wife's special fry-ups!
Poached eggs, bacon, sausages, orange
juice, coffee, buttered toast, mushrooms,
fried bread, grilled tomatoes, beans … "

"Have you got a wife then?" interrupted Arthur.

"Yes, and she's the bee's knees. In fact, she must be worrying herself stupid about where I am. So listen, it's been a great pleasure meeting you, but I must fly ..."

"Hold on!" said Arthur. "Don't I get a wish for setting you free?"

"Ooops!" said the genie, putting his hand over his mouth. "I forgot. Of course you do!"

He took a deep breath, turned a slightly

darker shade of green and said,

"*My freedom came by your brave hand*
And now your wish is my command!"

"Cool!" said Arthur. "Can I wish for anything?"

"Anything you like," said the genie, "but make it snappy because my tummy's rumbling like a hippopotamus that's just had its tail bitten by a crocodile."

Arthur thought for a moment. Then he said, "I don't really know what to wish for."

"Well, a chest of gold is a safe bet," said the genie. "Or … I can do you an apple that cures all known illnesses. Or a camel that never grows tired. How about that?"

Arthur wrinkled up his nose. "What I'd really like is my own video-messaging mobile phone," he said.

"Your own video-messaging mobile phone?" said the genie. "Are you sure you don't want the camel? It's got big humps and good teeth."

"No," said Arthur. "I don't want a camel."

"All right," said the genie, lowering his eyebrows. "Your own video-messaging mobiiiiiiiiiiile phoooooone it is!" And with that he started to wiggle his finger in the air.

"Wait!" said Arthur. "I want it to have a funky ringtone!"

"All right!" winked the genie. "A mobile phone with a fuuuuuunky ringtone!"

"And a magic button on the side that makes you invisible if you press it."

19

"What?" said the genie.

"And a magic button on the side that makes you invisible if you press it," repeated Arthur.

"A mobile phone can't make you invisible," said the genie.

"Yes it can," said Arthur. "I've just been watching a film on the telly all about one."

"Ah, that's the telly," said the genie with a little chuckle that became a cough. "Real life isn't like the telly! I can get you a mobile phone with a funky ringtone, no problem. But they don't come with magic invisible buttons."

"Mmm," said Arthur. "Maybe I'll wish for something else then."

"Well, make up your mind," tutted the genie. "I've got a long journey."

"Where do you live?" asked Arthur.

"Where do I live? Well, have you ever noticed there's one green star in the sky?"

Arthur shook his head.

"Not many people have," nodded the genie. "Anyway, that's where I live. Now make your wish! Make it good! And make it quick!"

21

"I know what I want," said Arthur. "I want you to build me a tree-house, like Warren's or a bit better."

"You want me to build you a tree-house?" said the genie. "What about that camel? It's very well-behaved."

"No!" said Arthur. "I don't want a camel. I want you to build me a tree-house."

"I don't know how to do that sort of thing," said the genie.

"Why not?"

"Well … genies just don't do that sort of thing. I don't have any tools or anything."

"My dad's got some!" said Arthur.

"Aah-haah!" smiled the genie. "I've got it. Why don't you wish for your dad to build the tree-house for you?"

"Oh, he doesn't know how to," shrugged Arthur. "He doesn't even know how to change a light-bulb."

"Well, I can change him," said the genie.

Arthur shook his head. "Even if you do, Dad's scared of heights. He won't be able to do it."

"He will," said the genie.

"He won't," said Arthur.

"How old are you?" asked the genie.

"Nine and a bit," said Arthur.

"Well I'm nine thousand and a bit. So shut up and trust me or I'm going to give you that camel and disappear in a puff of smoke!"

"All right, all right!" said Arthur. "I wish for my dad to build me a tree-house like Warren's or a bit better."

"A treeeeeeeeee-house it is!" winked the genie, wiggling his finger in the air.

"And one other thing!" added Arthur.

"What now?" sighed the genie, puffing out his cheeks.

"I want the tree-house to stop my mum and dad arguing."

"That's two wishes," said the genie. "Now you're being greedy!"

"Don't you know
how to do it then?"

"Of course I do," said the
genie. "I can make any wish
come true just as long as it
doesn't have to have a magic
invisible button on the side."

"Then make my mum and dad stop arguing, or I'm going to wish for you to build the tree-house."

"All right! All right! I'll do it for you!" said the genie, taking a deep breath. He wiggled his finger in the air and said, "*Harmunderjarmunderchoomunderchoo!*"

"Bless you," said Arthur.

"That wasn't a sneeze," tutted the genie. "That was a magic word. And it means that *your wish has come true*. Now I'm off to see my beautiful wife!"

With that he began to turn back into a puff of green smoke.

"She might not be so beautiful after nine thousand years!" called Arthur.

"Oh, don't spoil it," said the genie.

And he was gone.

CHAPTER 3
As Solid as a Rock

Arthur walked back up the road, not very sure what had just happened and even less sure what was going to happen next. At the house, Dad was still sitting on the up-turned box in the doorway of the garage. When he saw Arthur, he got to his feet and walked over to the pile of junk.

"You know what, Arthur," he said, picking up one of the planks. "If we were clever we'd do something with this stuff rather than just chuck it all out. I mean, these planks would be just the thing for a tree-house."

Arthur's eyes widened.

"But you said you didn't know how to build a tree-house!"

"Well," shrugged Dad, "all it really takes is a bit of imagination, some nails, and a tree. What do you reckon? Shall we give it a go?"

"If you say so."

"That's my boy!" grinned Dad, handing Arthur a plank. "You take this and I'll get the stepladder."

Dad disappeared into the garage, then came out with a toolbox in one hand and the stepladder over his shoulder.

"I thought you said that ladder was as wobbly as a jellyfish!" said Arthur.

"This?" said Dad, slapping the ladder. "It's as solid as a rock!"

Then he set off down the garden.

"What sort of tree-house are we going to

make?" called Arthur, wobbling after him
with the plank.

"Well," said Dad. "I thought it might be
like Warren's, only a bit better."

Arthur's face wrinkled into a smile. Then
he looked up at the great high branches of
the tree at the end of the garden and began
to wonder if he'd made such a sensible
wish after all.

"But Dad, you're scared of heights," pointed out Arthur.

Dad stood the stepladder next to the tree, then he looked up at branches high above.

"Sometimes," he said, "you've just got to go ahead and do what you're scared of. That's when you find out it's not so scary after all."

Then he strode off up the garden, whistling.

Back in the garage, Arthur sat down on a paint-pot as Dad spent a long time picking up bits of wood and checking them with a tape measure.

"Right, Arthur," he said. "Don't just sit there. Put some nails in your pockets and help me carry this stuff. We're going to need the rest of the planks, this coil of rope, those boards, and that tarpaulin. We'll fit this little window into one side, and what about a door?"

"There's a cupboard door over there, look," said Arthur.

31

"Good thinking," said Dad walking over to the old cupboard door. "Just the thing."

Once they had carried everything down the garden, Dad tucked a hammer into his belt and the two of them began to lift the first plank up the tree. The stepladder jiggled and wobbled as they climbed up it, but Dad didn't seem to notice.

Dad showed Arthur how to hold the hammer and hit the nails hard on the head. He hammered in the main ones, then he let Arthur do the last few. Within moments the plank was firmly nailed between the branches of the tree.

The two of them fetched the second plank, then the third and the fourth.

Arthur couldn't believe his eyes as his dad skipped up and down the creaky old ladder. But in no time at all, the floor of the tree-house was ready.

"Now," said Dad, rocking on his heels to test the strength of the planks. "You wait at the bottom of the ladder. We're going to hoist up those boards."

Arthur wobbled down the stepladder. Dad secured one end of a rope to a high branch and dropped the other end down. Arthur grabbed the rope and tied it round the boards so that Dad could pull them up.

They bracketed the walls to the floor, fitted the window and the door, and then tacked the tarpaulin over the top. The tree-house was ready! It seemed the whole thing had taken less time to make than the cheese sandwiches.

"That's amazing," said Arthur, sitting down on the little verandah around the outside of the tree-house. "It's finished!"

"Just one thing missing," said Dad, wiping a trickle of sweat from his forehead. "Hold on."

With that, he grabbed the rope to steady himself, dropped down onto the ladder and went striding back towards the house.

The sun was sinking in the sky, a warm breeze came through the leaves and Arthur felt on top of the world.

Moments later, Dad was back carrying a big bundle.

"Take this." He smiled as he came wobbling up the ladder. Arthur grabbed the bundle. Dad steadied himself on the rope and pulled himself up into the tree-house. But as he did, one of his shoelaces got caught in the hinge of the stepladder.

"Ooops!" said Dad with one knee on the tree-house, one hand on the rope, and one foot in mid-air. He yanked his foot up. But instead of freeing the shoelace, the whole ladder lifted off the ground.

"Woooooah!" said Dad, gripping with all his strength as the weight of the ladder made his hand slip down the rope.

"Hold on!" said Arthur, reaching down and trying to grab his leg, but it was too late. Dad swung away on the rope, with the ladder still dangling from his foot. He kicked up and down, and suddenly his shoelace snapped. The ladder toppled sideways and hit the ground with a great clunk

Dad looked down, and when he saw there was nothing underneath him, he wriggled his legs madly, trying to get a foothold on the tree-trunk. But he just got his foot tangled in the rope.

"Pull yourself up!" said Arthur.

"I can't," said Dad. "I'm stuck. You're going to have to call the fire-brigade."

"How?" said Arthur. "I'm stuck too."

Dad let out a groan and reached down to see if his phone was in his pocket. But, as he did, he lost his grip on the rope and toppled backwards.

"DAD!" called Arthur. But it was too late. With eyes as wide as windows, Dad clutched at air and fell away from the rope.

Arthur couldn't bear to look. He put his hand up to his face and waited for the terrible thud as his dad landed in the flowerbed. But it didn't come. So he slowly took his hand away from his eyes and looked down …

40

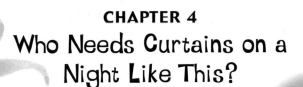

CHAPTER 4
Who Needs Curtains on a Night Like This?

Dad was still in mid-air, hanging upside down by one foot. It was tangled in the rope.

"Dad! Are you all right?" Arthur called.

"I'm walking on air," said Dad.

"I might be able to untangle your foot," called Arthur, reaching down.

"No! If you do I'll drop like a sack of potatoes."

At that moment, there was the sound of a car.

"Uh-oh!" whispered Arthur. "That's Mum."

"I know," said Dad.

"She's going to be hopping mad," said Arthur. "There's junk all over the front garden and you're hanging upside down from a tree."

"I know," repeated Dad. "She's going to be like a crocodile with toothache."

They heard the front door bang shut. Then Mum appeared at the back door, with the new living-room curtains draped over

her shoulder.

Mum spotted them up the tree and froze for a moment. Then she came racing down the garden.

Arthur thought she was going to look angry but, as she came closer, he saw her put her hand over her mouth to stop herself from laughing.

"What are you doing up there?" she asked.

"I'm waiting for a bus," said Dad, swaying gently from side to side. "It should be along any minute now …"

"You pair of bird-brains!" laughed Mum.

"Well, we decided to take your advice and get outdoors," said Arthur. "So we built this tree-house."

"I can see that," said Mum. "It looks lovely, but Dad seems to have got into a bit of a tangle on the way down."

"Very funny," said Dad. "Now why don't you do something to help?"

"All right," said Mum, bending down and propping up the stepladder.

Then she started to climb it with the living-room curtains still draped over her shoulder. Near the top, she reached out a hand and Dad grabbed it.

"Pull him over," called Arthur. "Then I can untangle his foot!"

Mum pulled. The ladder swayed. Dad grabbed the side of it.

Then there was a terrible crack as the stepladder split in two. The half of the ladder Dad had grabbed fell one way, and the half with Mum on it fell the other.

"Aaargh!" shouted Dad.

"No!" yelled Arthur.

"Ohhhh!" cried Mum, throwing her arms in the air and wrapping them round a branch of the tree.

The broken stepladder crashed to the ground with a dusty thud, and Mum swung her legs so that her feet were on another branch.

"Help!" she said.

"How?" asked Dad, running a hand through his upside-down hair.

Arthur knew it was up to him. He racked his brains for what to do next, and, almost as if by magic, it came to him.

"Look," he said. "We've got to let down a second rope. If we do that, Dad can hold on to it while I untangle his foot. Then he can slide down one and I can slide down the other."

"Good thinking," said Dad, "except we haven't got a second rope."

"Well, we'll just have to make one," said Arthur.

There was silence for a moment.

"Those curtains would do if we tore them into thick strips," said Dad.

"My new curtains!" scowled Mum. Arthur looked down at her and said, "Mum, what's more important, Dad or the living-room curtains?"

"Well ..." said Mum after a moment's thought. "Dad ... just."

So Mum swivelled round on the branch and tossed the curtains up to Arthur. He started tearing them into strips, then knotted the strips tightly together.

Then he tied the curtain-rope to the branch and dropped it down.

"It'll be curtains for me if it breaks," muttered Dad, reaching out and gripping it with both hands.

"Right," said Arthur. "I'm going to climb a little way down this rope so that I can untangle your foot."

"Be careful!" called Mum.

Arthur's stomach lurched as he swung out into the air, but he breathed deeply and edged his way down the rope until he was right above Dad's foot. He reached down and tugged at the rope. Dad's foot came free and he swung off onto the second rope.

When the two of them were only a few feet off the ground, they let themselves drop from the ropes.

"That's my boy!" said Dad, giving Arthur a hug. "Bold as a lion, just like his father!"

"What about me?" asked Mum.

"We've got to fix this ladder," said Arthur, picking up the hammer and nails.

"Hold on."

"I don't think I *can* hold on!" said Mum.

"Then jump!" said Dad. "I'll catch you!"

"You must be joking," she said.

"Trust me!"

So Dad held out his arms. Arthur held his breath. And Mum launched herself off the branch. Down she dropped, straight into Dad's arms.

"I may not be much good at changing light-bulbs," said Dad, "but when it comes to catching the woman I love, I'm the best!"

"Let's go in and put the kettle on."

"Good idea," nodded Dad. But then he put a hand up to his forehead and said, "Wait a minute … we can't."

"Why?" asked Arthur.

"Because the kettle's up there in that bundle I gave you. The tea's up there, and the chocolate biscuits, and the milk and our camping-stove."

They all looked up at the tree-house. It was getting dark, and one or two stars were glinting in the blue-black sky.

"Well, you've got to go back up," said Mum. "You can't just leave our kettle up in the tree-house."

"Don't worry," said Arthur, standing the ladder up. "Look, I've fixed it."

"I don't care what you've done to it," said Dad. "I nearly met a fate worse than death up there, and I'm not going back –

not even for a packet of chocolate biscuits."

"I thought you were meant to be as bold as a lion!" said Arthur.

He looked at his Dad, then added, "Look. What I really want is *all three* of us to go back up the tree and have tea and chocolate biscuits up there."

Arthur looked at Mum. Mum looked at Dad. And Dad looked at the ladder.

"Hmm … are you sure this ladder's safe?" he said.

"As solid as a rock," said Arthur.

"How did you learn to hammer nails like that?" asked Dad.

"You taught me," said Arthur. "Now let's all go up and have those chocolate biscuits."

With that, Arthur climbed the ladder and pulled himself up into the tree-house. Mum followed slowly. Dad even more slowly.

The peppery smell of the tree filled the warm night air and, high above, a great stretch of stars reached across the sky.

"It's nice up here," said Mum, taking a deep breath.

"Beautiful," said Dad, taking a chocolate

biscuit. "Who needs curtains on a night like this?"

Arthur couldn't tell if Mum was glaring or smiling at him. In any case, the kettle whistled on the little camping stove and Dad said he'd make the tea.

As the three of them drank their tea, Arthur looked up at the sky. Far to one side of it, something caught his eye. It was a tiny green star. And, as he looked at it, he could have sworn it winked at him.

From then on, Arthur, Mum and Dad quite often climbed up the tree to have tea and biscuits together. Of course, Mum and Dad did sometimes have arguments. But, you know, they never once did when they were up in that tree-house.